MAGIC KEEPERS

TUNNEL TROUBLE

LINDA CHAPMAN
Illustrated by Hoang Giang

LITTLE TIGER
LONDON

MAGIC KEEPERS

TUNNEL TROUBLE

For Bracken and Blossom, my two Tibetan terriers
who give me new ideas for Pepper every day! - L.C.

To JK, for teaching me that every little
effort counts – H. G.

LITTLE TIGER
An imprint of Little Tiger Press Limited
1 Coda Studios, 189 Munster Road, London SW6 6AW

Imported into the EEA by Penguin Random House Ireland,
Morrison Chambers, 32 Nassau Street, Dublin D02 YH68

A paperback original
First published in Great Britain in 2023

Text copyright © Linda Chapman, 2023
Illustration copyright © Hoang Giang, 2023

ISBN: 978-1-78895-478-5

A CIP catalogue record for this book is available from the British Library.

Printed and bound in the UK.

MIX
Paper | Supporting
responsible forestry
FSC® C171272

The Forest Stewardship Council® (FSC®) is a global, not-for-profit organization
dedicated to the promotion of responsible forest management worldwide. FSC defines
standards based on agreed principles for responsible forest stewardship that are supported
by environmental, social, and economic stakeholders. To learn more, visit www.fsc.org

10 9 8 7 6 5 4 3 2 1

CONTENTS

CHAPTER ONE

Ten magic crystals glimmered as they nestled in their individual compartments in the old leather box on the desk. Watched eagerly by her best friends Lily and Sarah and her dog Pepper, Ava moved her hand over the top, her palm not quite touching the crystals. She could feel them all faintly vibrating. Some released sharp pulses of energy, others were long and soothing or tingly and tickly. Excitement swept through her. Which one should she do magic with? The soft pink Rose Quartz? The glowing green Jade?

Ava's stomach fizzed at the thought of doing magic. She could still hardly believe how much her life had changed in the last six weeks. She and her mum had moved house, she'd started a new school and she'd met Lily and Sarah. But best of all she'd made the amazing discovery that magic was real!

It had all begun when Ava's mum had inherited Curio House and its contents from her great-aunt Enid who had been a famous archaeologist. Curio House was a huge, crumbling Victorian villa with eight bedrooms and a large walled garden, and in one of the rooms there was a collection of unusual old objects called curios. Ava, Lily and Sarah had found out that all the curios were magic in some way and that Great-Aunt Enid had been keeping their magic secret. The girls were determined to keep it secret too. The last thing they wanted was someone taking the collection away!

However, it wasn't always easy. First, a baby crocodile mummy had come to life and they'd had to catch it after it escaped from the house. Then, an ancient nature spirit had left its stone plaque to cause chaos in town, making plants and trees grow everywhere, until they managed to trap it and send it back to sleep. Being magic keepers was a lot of fun but it was also a lot of work!

Along with the curios, Great-Aunt Enid had left a box of *'Magyck Crystals for the Protection of the Magyck Curios'*. The girls had used the crystals to help in their last two adventures but they were still finding out how the crystals worked.

They had decided to go to Ava's house after school that day to practise controlling the magic.

Ava's fingers paused as they passed over a dark grey stone with patches of deep red. She felt like the stone was reaching out to her, urging her to use it. "I'm going to try this one," she announced, picking it up.

"That's the Bloodstone. We used it when we first discovered the crystals were magic," said Lily, pushing her hair behind her ears. She and Sarah were cousins but they looked very different – Lily had shiny black hair and dark brown eyes whereas Sarah had chin-length blonde hair and blue eyes. They had very different personalities too.

Lily now picked up the box. Great-Aunt Enid had written notes about the crystals on the inside of the lid in her tiny, cramped handwriting. "*Bloodstone,*" she read out. "*The Enhancing Crystal. Bloodstone increases energy and courage. It enhances physical powers and decision-making.*"

Sarah had a notebook ready and a pen in her hand. "Why did you choose that particular crystal, Ava?" She was very scientific and loved finding things out.

Ava shrugged. It was like trying to explain why you liked one colour more than another. "It just felt right."

"But why exactly?" pressed Sarah. "Can you be more specific?"

"Nope," said Ava. She couldn't explain it but some things just felt right or wrong. Sometimes she sensed something bad was about to happen, or she could instinctively tell if a person or animal was ill or in trouble. Her mum said it was because she was very intuitive. It seemed to make it easy for her to do magic – the crystals always worked more quickly for her than for the others.

Sarah made a note. "OK, so, now you've picked it, why don't you see how well you can control the magic?"

Ava focused on the crystal, letting everything else fade away – the high-ceilinged room with its dusty bookcases and shelves full of curios; the huge sash windows framed by velvet curtains; the faded rugs on the wooden floor and the old sofas. Even her friends and her Tibetan terrier Pepper – who was lying on a chair watching her through her shaggy fringe – disappeared. Ava felt the crystal's energy merging with hers and she caught her breath.

"What is it?" asked Sarah, her pen poised.

"I feel strong and brave, like I could do anything!" she said as the magic flowed into her.

"Try putting the crystal in the necklace," said Lily, handing Ava a gold necklace from the box. It had a triangular pendant hanging from it. In each corner of the triangle there was a small, clear crystal and in the centre was an empty, round gap. The girls had discovered that when a crystal was put inside the pendant, the crystal's power grew even stronger. Ava fitted the Bloodstone to it and the gem started to sparkle brightly. She slipped the chain over her head, pulling out her thick chestnut hair from underneath and settling it around her neck.

"Oh … my … wow!" she exclaimed as energy swept through her like a tidal wave. Ava felt a wild urge to race around the room but instead of giving in to the urge, she held on to the energy, feeling it fill every cell in her body.

"I've got control of the magic," she breathed.

It buzzed inside her, making her feel she was full of fizzing bubbles. She focused on what she wanted to use it for and then threw herself into a cartwheel but instead of just doing one like she would normally do, she did another and then another until she had cartwheeled all the way round the room.

She heard the gasps of the others and leaped into a karate stance. She loved karate and was a brown belt. She began to move through one of her *katas* – a set routine that showed off kicks and punches. She moved at lightning speed, the energy soaring through her, pushing her on. She'd never done karate so well! One *kata* merged effortlessly into another until she felt like she was just a blur of movement. Her punches had never been sharper, her kicks higher, her spins faster. With a final *kiai* – a deep yell – she stopped. She was panting but elated. Sarah had been so engrossed she'd even stopped making notes and Lily's mouth was hanging open.

"That was incredible, Ava!" she exclaimed. "You were like Super Girl."

"Or Karate Kid," said Sarah, her eyes wide.

Pepper had jumped off the chair and was bouncing round Ava excitedly.

Ava's brown eyes shone. "I love this crystal! Here, why don't one of you try it? Lily, how about you? You could see if you've also got better at controlling its magic?"

"OK," Lily said eagerly.

She put the necklace on and after a moment, she gasped. "Oh, gosh! I don't think I have!" She started to jog on the spot, getting faster and faster.

"Try and control the energy," advised Ava,

remembering what she'd done. "See if you can hold it inside you and focus on how you want to use it…"

"I … I can't!" Lily spluttered. Jumping into the air, she started to do ballet wildly around the room. She cat-leaped and pirouetted, took off in a grand jeté but mistimed her landing and collapsed on her tummy on the floor, laughing. Pepper leaped on top of her in excitement, licking her nose.

"Ew! Pepper!" Lily giggled, pushing the terrier away. "Enough with the doggy kisses!" She pulled the necklace off and sighed with relief. "That was the weirdest feeling! I don't know how you controlled the energy, Ava. I just couldn't. I wasn't Super Girl or Karate Kid, I was more like Ballet Flop!"

They snorted with laughter. "Why don't you try, Sarah?" Lily said.

Sarah put down her notebook and slipped the necklace on.

"Well?" Ava asked eagerly.

Sarah frowned. "I'm not feeling anything."

"Maybe it's because you've not connected to the crystal yet," said Ava. "Open your mind to it. Don't think about anything else. Focus on it but don't try too hard."

"You've got this, Sarah," Lily encouraged. "You can do it."

Sarah shut her eyes. After a few moments, she shook her head. "Nope," she said, frustrated.

"Nothing's happening."

"I'm sure it'll work soon," said Lily soothingly. "Or you could try a different crystal, maybe that one's just not right for you."

"That's it!" Ava said suddenly. "Lily, you've got it!"

"I have?" Lily looked surprised. "What?"

"Sarah asked me earlier why I chose the Bloodstone and I said it was because it just felt right to me. But maybe it's not the right crystal for Sarah."

Lily looked excited. "Ooh, there might be a better one for me too," she said. "One I can actually control."

"Try," Ava urged them. She glanced at the old clock on the wall. "We've still got time before your mums come to collect you."

Sarah took the necklace off and put the Bloodstone back, then she and Lily ran their hands over the top of the crystals in the box like Ava had done. Almost immediately, Lily picked out a pink crystal. "This one! Rose Quartz." She read out the notes on the box. "*Rose Quartz: the Peace Crystal. Rose Quartz restores and balances and promotes love.*" She smiled. "It's making my fingers tingle and me all warm and happy. I feel like I would know just the right words to comfort someone or make them feel better. It just feels so … so *right*!"

"I don't get it," said Sarah. "What do you mean, it feels … wait!" She broke off, her hand hovering over a deep blue crystal. Her eyes flew to the others' faces. "My fingers just tingled."

"Pick that one up!" Lily said in delight.

"Hold on," said Ava, suddenly. "That's Lapis Lazuli, the Truth Crystal. Do you remember the time when we held it, Lily? Before Sarah knew about the magic? It made us tell the truth."

It was back when they had first discovered the crystals were magic and it hadn't been a nice feeling at all. Ava hadn't been able to control what she was saying. She'd confessed to Lily about how she was sad she didn't see her dad much – he lived in Scotland – and how she sometimes felt jealous of her half-brother – her dad's new baby son. When Lily had held the crystal she told Ava that her younger brother and sister always seemed to get what they wanted and she always had to give way to keep the peace.

Lily looked alarmed. "I didn't like that crystal at all."

"Well?" said Sarah, her hand hovering over it. "Should I try it?"

Pepper pricked her ears and ran to the door with a woof. They heard Ava's mum in the hall, opening the front door.

"Cai! Come in. The girls are around somewhere. Have you got time for a cup of tea?"

"That would be lovely," they heard Cai, Lily's mum, reply. "If you don't mind Huy and Mai joining us!" Huy and Mai were Lily's younger brother and sister. Huy was two and Mai was five.

"Of course not! Come in, all of you," said Ava's mum.

"Auntie Cai's here," said Sarah, her face falling. "We'll have to stop now."

"We can carry on tomorrow after school," said Ava. "You can use the Truth Crystal then, Sarah – if you really want to."

"I definitely do!" said Sarah. "We need to know how to use all of the crystals in case we have to protect the curios again."

Ava glanced at the dusty curios. Which would be the next one to cause trouble? The curse cup?

The figurine with the cat head and evil eyes? The stone gargoyle with its fierce expression, folded wings and clawed hands? The fan of greying ostrich feathers, or the brooch in the shape of a scarab beetle that had a bird with outstretched wings engraved on its back?

"Girls!" Ava's mum called. "Lily's mum is here!"

"Coming!" Ava shouted. She shut the lid of the crystal box and they hurried out of the room.

CHAPTER TWO

Huy and Mai were taking their boots off in the hall. "Ava!" said Mai, hugging her. She had chin-length hair that was held to one side with a sparkly pink hairslide.

"Hi, Mai!" said Ava, hugging her back. Mai was in Reception class at school. She liked to play with Lily and the others at breaktime and lunchtime. At first it had just been occasionally, but Ava was so good at making up games Mai now wanted to play with them all the time.

Pepper trotted over to say hello. Mai stroked

her and Pepper stuck her nose in Mai's face, making her giggle.

Huy sneezed. Cai scooped him up, swinging him on to her hip. "Sorry, he's allergic to dogs," she explained. "He sneezes if he gets too close."

"Come through to the kitchen, then," said Fran. "I'll get the kids some biscuits then the girls can take Pepper."

Ava felt a surge of hope. Maybe they would have some more time with the crystals after all? "I'll go with the big girls," said Mai quickly. "I like Pepper and I'm not allergic." She slipped her hand into Ava's. "We can play some games."

"Or you could stay with Mum?" Lily suggested.

Mai frowned. "No. I want to come with you."

"OK, then," Lily sighed.

"Yay!" Mai gave a little skip.

Lily shot an apologetic look at the others as they followed Cai and Fran into the kitchen. "Sorry," she mouthed.

"It's OK," Ava mouthed back over Mai's head.

It would have been fun to do more with the crystals but it probably wasn't sensible with both their mums there. She grinned as she imagined the shock on their faces if they saw her in super-speed karate mode or Lily doing her wild ballet!

Fran put the kettle on while Cai sat down at the pine table. "The kitchen's looking lovely now you've finished decorating."

Fran laughed. "Thanks! Pity about the rest of the house. I'll get there in the end, though."

"How old is the house?" asked Cai as Fran got a big selection box of biscuits from the cupboard and started offering them round.

"Almost two hundred years but there are some older sections that date way back. It used to be the local carrier's cottage – the person who transported goods in and out of the town using a horse and cart – but then it burned down in a fire in 1845 and this house was built in its place. The old carrier's cellar where the goods were kept is still under the house." Fran waved at a couple of stone steps in one corner of the kitchen that led down to a little door in the wall. "I had a quick look when we first moved in but there were far too many spiders there for me!"

"You're so lucky to live here," said Cai. "I find old buildings fascinating. All that history..."

Ava motioned with her eyes to the door. If the mums were going to start going on about history she wanted to get out of there!

"I wanna biscuit!" Lily's little brother Huy

said, pointing at Fran as she offered Mai a biscuit. "Wanna biscuit NOW!"

"Wait your turn and say please, Huy," Cai said.

He shook his head. "No."

Cai looked embarrassed. "Sorry. He's going through a difficult stage."

Huy's voice grew louder. "Biscuit!" He looked at Ava's mum and very reluctantly added. "Peas."

"Here you go," said Fran offering him the box. Huy shook his head and pointed at Lily's jammy dodger. "DAT biscuit."

"No, Huy, that's Lily's biscuit and there are none of those left," said his mum. "Choose another."

Huy started to frown. "Want DAT one!"

"It's OK, Mum, he can have it," said Lily quickly, holding the biscuit out to her little brother. "Say please, though."

"Peas," Huy muttered.

Lily handed the biscuit over and took a

different one from the box.

"Thanks, love," Lily's mum said gratefully.

Ava saw Pepper eyeing up the biscuit in Huy's hand and grabbed her collar just in time. Pepper wriggled round and in a flash she'd grabbed the jammy dodger from Ava's other hand. It was gone in two gulps! "Pepper!" Ava exclaimed.

Pepper licked the crumbs from her nose, looking very smug.

"You'd better take her out of here," said Ava's mum as Huy sneezed again.

The girls trooped out. As they went into the hall, Mai looked inquisitively at the big oak door that led into the Curio Room. "What's in there?"

"All kinds of special things." Ava could have kicked herself as she saw the little girl's eyes light up. "I mean boring old things," she said hastily.

"Very, very boring," said Lily quickly. "Nothing exciting at all."

"Just dusty objects and a lot of books," said Sarah.

"I like books," said Mai. "I want to see."

Ava jumped in front of her. "Wait! I've got a better idea. Why don't we go into the lounge and we can play a game. Anything you want."

Mai's face lit up. "OK! Let's do a play! I'll be the princess. You can be a dragon alien monster," she said pointing to Sarah. "You can be the prince, Lily, and Ava can be a wizard."

For the next twenty minutes, Mai bossed them all around, telling them what to do and say. The older girls didn't enjoy it very much but they went along with it to keep Mai happy.

"Do you want to do something else now, Mai?" said Ava after she'd cast what felt like

her hundredth spell making Mai the most
beautiful princess in the land. "How about
lion and mouse?" She'd made up a game in the
playground at school which involved them being
lions and Mai being a mouse.

Mai nodded eagerly.

"We'll count to twenty," Ava told Mai,
holding Pepper's collar.

Mai ran off.

"Sorry we're having to play with her," Lily
whispered.

"It is a bit of a pain," said Sarah honestly.

Ava saw Lily's face fall. "It's fine," she said
quickly. "I'll show her my bedroom or teach her
to do some karate next. She always likes that."

"Thanks," Lily said gratefully.

They began to hunt around, pretending to
be lions. "We're coming to get you!" Ava called.
"We want a nice little mousie for our supper."

"RARRR!" said Lily. "We're going to find
you, Mai!"

They heard a very faint giggle from the direction of the hall. "Where is she?" whispered Sarah.

"RARRRRRRR!" Ava roared, going into the hall.

There was another giggle.

The Curio Room door was open. Ava's heart sank. She should have guessed that Mai would go in there!

She ran inside. One of the long velvet curtains that hung at the sides of the large middle window near the shelves of curios moved and Ava saw a Mai-sized bump behind it.

Ava charged towards it. "Got you!" she said, pulling the curtain back. Mai squealed in delight, rolling around as Ava tickled her and pretended to gobble her up. "Yum! Yum! I like eating mousies!"

Mai wriggled away and noticed the curios. She ran over to them. "What's this?" she said, picking up the baby crocodile mummy.

"Don't touch that, Mai," said Ava hastily, taking it out of the little girl's hand and putting it back on the shelf. "In fact, don't touch anything," she said as Mai lifted up a dented goblet and pretended to drink from it. She and the others knew it didn't take much for the curios' magic to come to life.

"Mai, put those down," said Lily, her voice rising in panic as Mai looked into a tarnished silver mirror and combed her hair with an old tortoiseshell comb.

Mai did as she was told but then found a random white petal on one of the shelves and popped it into the gargoyle's open mouth. She giggled. "That monster's got a funny face."

"Seriously, Mai, please don't play with these things!" pleaded Sarah.

Lily tried to take her sister's hand but Mai pulled away from her and picked up the figurine with the cat head. "Look at this creepy cat person." She grabbed the beetle brooch with the bird carved into its back. "And what's this?"

"No and no!" said Sarah anxiously, plucking them out of her hands, one by one.

Ava saw Mai's mouth open and her face screw up. Oh no! There was a tantrum coming!

"Hey, Mai, why don't you come upstairs to my bedroom?" Ava suggested. She ran to the door while Sarah carefully put the brooch and the cat figurine back in the exact same positions they'd been in before. "You can play with my art things."

The storm cleared from Mai's face instantly. "OK!" she said eagerly. She ran past Ava and into the hall.

"That was close," whispered Ava as she and the others hurried upstairs after Mai.

*

Mai loved to paint and draw, and Ava had lots of art things because drawing was one of her favourite things to do too. She, Lily and Sarah drew pictures with the little girl using Ava's felt tips and pastels until Sarah's mum Ruth arrived.

"Hello, girls," said Ruth. She gave Ava a warm smile and, to Ava's delight, bent down and patted Pepper who Ava was holding on to. Ruth hadn't been very keen on Ava being friends with Sarah at first – and she'd been very wary of Pepper – but now she seemed to be warming to them both.

"Thank you for letting me come round and play," said Mai to Fran.

"No problem, sweetie," said Fran, helping her on with her coat.

"Where's your hairslide, love?" Cai said.

Mai's hand went to her head. Her slide was missing.

"It must have fallen out while we were playing," said Ava. "I'll go and see if I can find it." She ran back into the Curio Room and had a quick look around but couldn't see it.

"Don't worry, we've got others," said Cai as Ava came back empty-handed.

"But I like that one," said Mai, pouting.

"You can have one of my slides instead," said Lily quickly. "How about the one with the dolphin on?"

Mai instantly cheered up and ran outside, jumping down the steps.

"You're such a lovely big sister," Fran said to Lily.

"She is, isn't she?" said Cai, giving Lily a quick hug. "Lily's so wonderful. I don't know what I'd do without her."

Lily smiled happily.

"Time to go, Sarah. You have music practice before bed," said Ruth.

They all said goodbye and as Ava shut the door, she breathed out loudly.

"That's a big sigh," her mum said, giving her a quizzical look.

"I am VERY glad I don't have little brothers and sisters!" Ava said. Pepper woofed and jumped around her. Ava grinned and crouched down to hug her. "Pepper's more than enough for me!"

*

That night when Ava went to bed, she added an extra fleece throw over her duvet. It was a very cold night and the heating in Curio House never worked that well. While Ava brushed her hair, Pepper jumped on to the bed and curled up right in the middle of it.

"Move, Pepper!" said Ava, hurrying over and

wriggling under the covers. Pepper got up with a sigh to make room for Ava and then flopped down again. Ava wrapped her arms around the little dog and Pepper snuggled closer. It was like having a hairy hot-water bottle.

"It was fun using the crystals today," Ava whispered to her. She thought about how they had each found a crystal that felt right for them, the Bloodstone for her, the Rose Quartz for Lily and the Lapis Lazuli for Sarah. The Crystals of Energy, Peace and Truth. "I guess we each picked a crystal that's like us," she said to Pepper. She was very energetic, Lily was very good at keeping the peace and Sarah was very truthful. Maybe the crystals felt right to them because they reflected their personalities and that was why they found those particular crystals easy to use...

She was just drifting off to sleep when she thought she heard a faint rattle.

Pepper lifted her head and growled.

"Did you hear something too?" Ava said,

sitting up. She listened hard but didn't hear anything else.

Pepper jumped off the bed and trotted to the window, standing up on her back legs and staring out into the night. She let out a sharp bark. Ava felt a shiver of unease run down her spine and joined her at the window, the chilly air biting her bare feet. Peering out into the dark, she looked down into the shadowy garden but it was still and quiet. Her unease faded. "There's nothing there," she said.

Pepper raced back to the bed. She leaped straight into the warm spot Ava had just left and curled up like a doughnut, her eyes peeking out cheekily at Ava from under her fringe.

"Pepper!" Ava said indignantly. "Did you just woof to get me out of bed?" She ran back to her bed and wriggled in beside her. "You are so naughty," she told the little dog, kissing her head. "It's lucky I love you!"

Pepper rolled on her back and soon both she and Ava were fast asleep.

CHAPTER THREE

When Ava left for school the next morning there
was a thick coating of frost on the trees and the
puddles had frozen. Ava gave Pepper a last kiss
then set off for Lily's house.

Lily was waiting in the porch. "Let's go
before Mai asks if she can walk with us," she
said, glancing behind to where her mum was
strapping Huy into his buggy and Mai was
pulling her school bag on to her back.

They set off together. "I wonder how Sarah
will get on with the Truth Crystal later," said

Lily in a low voice.

Ava had been wondering the same thing. "I hope she's OK with it. I didn't like it when I held it and…" She broke off as something caught her attention. Behind the hedge they were walking past there was a hollow tower about eight metres tall with a window, and ivy creeping across its sides. There was an arched entrance in its base that was closed off by an iron grate, covered with brambles. Ava had never really taken much notice of it before but now, covered in a layer of frost, it looked like it was from a fairy tale.

41

"That's a peculiar building, isn't it?" she said, stopping to look at it. "What's it for? It's too small for anyone to live in."

"It's a folly, a kind of fake building that rich people used to build to impress their friends." Like her mum, Lily was keen on history. "It's really old. My dad told me it was built over the entrance to one of the tunnels that go under the town."

Ava was intrigued. She remembered Lily telling her about the maze of tunnels that ran under Eastwold. "What are they for?"

"No one's quite sure. They were built back in the 1200s. There's a network of natural caves and the tunnels connect them. Some people say they were used by smugglers, others that they were a way for people to keep safe in times of danger. Eastwold's supposed to be a place that attracts magic so maybe there was lots of dangerous magic around then!"

"Can you get into it?" Ava asked. "It would be

awesome to explore them!"

Lily shook her head. "There are a few entrances in the oldest buildings in town but they're all blocked off. People aren't allowed to go down there in case they get lost. There are rumours there are ghosts in the tunnels, ghosts of people who got trapped there and died." She shivered.

Ava grinned. "Ghosts aren't real."

"People say magic isn't real," Lily pointed out. "When we know it is."

Ava couldn't argue with that!

"Lily! Ava!" They looked round. While they'd been looking at the folly, Mai had caught up with them. "What are you talking about?"

"Nothing," the older girls said quickly. Mai took Ava's hand and they carried on walking.

"You look tired," Ava said, noticing Mai's face was paler than usual and she was yawning.

"A monster came to my window last night," Mai said. "It wanted to get in and eat me!"

Lily put an arm round her sister and hugged her. "Sounds like you had a horrible nightmare."

"It wasn't a nightmare," said Mai, pouting.

Lily swapped quick smiles with Ava. "Well, next time the monster comes, Mai, get me and I'll scare it away."

"OK," said Mai, looking happier.

There was the sound of shouting and two boys who looked like twins came flying past on their scooters. Laughing, they swerved around the girls, narrowly missing them. A few seconds later their dad came scootering past. "Wait, boys!" he panted.

Mai scowled. "That's Joe and Isaac," she said. "I don't like them. They're in my class and they're mean."

She stepped on a frozen puddle and skidded.

"Careful, Mai!" Lily warned.

"It's fun!" said Mai, pretending to ice skate on the frozen puddle. "Look at me … ow!" she gasped as she fell over.

"Oh, Mai!" groaned Lily, helping her up. "Are you OK?"

Out of the corner of her eye, Ava caught sight of a movement in the hedge right by them. Was it an animal? She looked more closely but whatever it was had vanished into the undergrowth.

"Come on," said Lily. "We don't want to be late."

Ava joined them, and holding firmly on to Mai's hand so she didn't fall over again, they continued on to school.

*

Sarah was in a different class to Ava and Lily.
She was in Year Five while they were in Year
Six, although secretly Ava thought that Sarah
was cleverer than anyone in their class. She
had a great memory and loved learning facts,
particularly science ones. Being in different
classes meant that their only chance of hanging
out together and talking about magic was
at break and lunchtime. But that day, as
they found each other in the noisy, crowded
playground, Mai came running over to them
too. "What are we going to play today?" she
asked.

Ava really wanted a chance to talk about the
crystals. Looking at Sarah and Lily's faces she
could see they felt the same. "Why don't you go
and play with some of your friends today?" she
suggested.

"I don't have any friends," said Mai.

"Don't be silly," said Lily. "You do."

"You like Cici, don't you?" Ava pointed to another little girl in Reception who was standing by herself. "She looks like she needs someone to play with."

"I want to play with you!" said Mai stubbornly.

"OK, then," Lily sighed.

But Sarah frowned. "Listen, Mai," she said, her voice kind but firm. "We like playing with you but not all the time, and we would like some time on our own now."

Mai's face started to screw up as if she was about to have a tantrum. "I'll tell Mummy you wouldn't let me play with you!" she said to Lily, her voice rising.

"OK, OK, calm down, we can play with you, Mai," Lily said quickly.

Mai's face broke into a smile. "Yay! Let's play mouse and lions! You count to twenty!" She raced away.

Sarah gave Lily an exasperated look. "Why do you always give in to her? You should tell her to play with her own friends some of the time."

"But I don't want to be mean," protested Lily.

"I know, but she needs to make friends her own age," Sarah said. "And you shouldn't always have to do everything she wants. What you want matters too, you know."

Lily shrugged. "It's fine. I really don't mind."

But Ava knew that wasn't true. She remembered what Lily had said when they used the Truth Crystal.

Lily glanced in the direction Mai had gone. "Listen, if you two don't want to play with her, that's OK. I'll be fine on my own."

"Don't be silly," said Ava quickly. "We'll all play and we can talk about magic later."

"And do it!" added Sarah.

They grinned at each other and then ran to find Mai.

*

After school, Mai insisted on walking with Ava, Lily and Sarah, rather than with her mum and Huy in his buggy. She skipped along beside them.

"I've got a spelling test tomorrow. I don't like spelling tests."

"Me neither," said Ava. She was good at maths and very good at art but she found reading and writing hard. The words jumped around when she tried to read so she had to go very slowly and she could never remember how to spell anything no matter how hard she tried. Luckily, Lily helped her.

"Today, we played in the sand and made a

model with boxes. Mine's a spaceship!" she said. "Joe and Isaac knocked it over and it broke but Mrs Jelson helped me fix it."

Just then the twins came racing past on their scooters. One of them came so close to Mai, he bumped into her bag.

"Whoops! Sorry, Mai!" he laughed.

"Be careful, boys!" exclaimed their dad as he scooted after them. "Sorry!" he called to the girls.

"They're going to knock someone over," said Sarah, frowning. "It's not safe. Their dad should make them go more slowly."

Ava heard a rustle in the hedge at the side of the pavement. Looking towards it, she caught a brief glimpse of an animal darting into the undergrowth. A faint prickle ran over her skin. She wondered if it was the same creature she'd seen that morning.

"Ava?" said Lily, looking back at her. "Are you coming?"

"Sure." Telling herself it was just a coincidence, Ava caught up with them.

When they reached Lily's house, Mai spotted their neighbour's large ginger cat sitting on the pavement. "Marmalade!" she cried, running over.

The cat meowed in protest as she hugged him.

"Don't squeeze him too tightly!" called Lily quickly. "You know he doesn't like…"

"Ow!" Mai cried as the cat scratched her. "He hurt me!"

Ava was very relieved when Cai caught up with them. She whisked Mai indoors to find her a plaster.

As the door shut on Mai's wails, Sarah breathed a sigh of relief. "Alone at last."

Ava grinned. "So, who's ready to do some magic?"

"Me!" Sarah and Lily exclaimed.

And they all linked arms and headed off to Ava's house.

CHAPTER FOUR

Pepper bounced around them when they arrived. As they were still wearing their coats, gloves and hats, they took Pepper out into the garden first. The little dog ran around and then bounded to the middle of the three large Curio Room windows. She stood on her back legs, putting her front paws on the wide stone windowsill and sniffed along it as if someone had put some sausages there.

Ava rubbed her hands together and stamped her feet. "Come, Peps, let's not stay out too long.

It's freezing!" she called, her breath turning into white clouds in the frosty air.

Pepper continued sniffing the sill, ignoring her completely.

"She's so naughty," Lily said with a giggle.

Ava ran over and picked Pepper up. "Come on, trouble. Let's go inside."

But as she carried the dog towards the house, Pepper looked over Ava's shoulder in the direction of the window and barked. Ava glanced round, suddenly remembering the way Pepper had growled in the night. It wasn't like her to bark or growl at thin air. The last time she'd acted like this had been when the crocodile mummy and nature spirit had escaped.

It's probably nothing, Ava told herself, but the thought niggled at her.

When she and the others went into the Curio Room, Pepper ran to sniff by the middle window and Ava made a beeline for the shelves. Were all the curios still there?

She had a brilliant memory and as she looked along the shelves she felt sure everything was still in the right place and her unease dropped a notch. Maybe Pepper was just being silly.

Sarah opened the box of crystals. "I can't wait to see if the Truth Crystal will work for me. *Lapis Lazuli encourages honesty,*" she read out. "*It brings forth the truth and finds those things that are hidden and lost. It also enhances memory.*" She took out the deep blue crystal. "Here goes."

Ava could still remember the feeling she'd had when she'd first held it, the way she'd suddenly found herself talking without being able to stop, her hidden thoughts bursting out of her. Her stomach twisted anxiously. Would the same happen to Sarah? She hoped the magic wouldn't make her say anything she would feel embarrassed about afterwards.

Lily seemed to be thinking the same thing. "You can always try a different crystal, Sarah…"

"No," Sarah interrupted, smiling as she cradled the crystal in her hands. "I like this one and I can already feel it working. It's like my head is swirling with energy. I feel as if I could remember anything."

"It's not making you want to start talking about stuff?" said Lily. "Say things you usually keep hidden?"

"No," said Sarah, looking surprised.

"I think I know why." Ava remembered what she'd been thinking the night before, about how they had each chosen a crystal that matched their personality. "Sarah tells the truth even when she's not holding the crystal so she doesn't have big secrets for the crystal to reveal."

"Do you think it can improve my memory?" said Sarah. "That would be amazing!"

"Your memory's incredible as it is," said Lily.

Sarah grinned. "Thanks, but it can always be better." She went over to the shelves and read the labels of the curios on the bottom shelf then she turned away and started to recite them out loud, word for word. *"Curse Cup. Nottingham. Circa 1505. Found in cellar of Lowdham Manor. Note the unusual carvings… Seeds of the extinct Afypnistis Flower, Ancient Greece. Note its seeds possess the ability to attract spirits and the petals to awaken them… Guardian Stone Gargoyle. Eastwold. Circa mid 1200s. Removed from church when it was renovated in 1810. Note open mouth to inspire fear in enemies… Saxon Boundary Stone. Norfolk…"*

She broke off. "This is awesome! I can see all the words I just read in my head. I don't even have to try to remember them."

"Why don't you put the crystal in the necklace?" Ava said. "See what happens then." She passed the necklace to Sarah who fitted the crystal into the pendant. The Lapis Lazuli started to glitter with a blue light.

"Oh, wow!" Sarah breathed as she put the necklace over her head. "The magic is even stronger now!" She jumped to her feet. "I wonder if I can use it to find something that's been lost."

"What about Mai's hairslide?" suggested Lily. "The one she lost yesterday."

Sarah nodded. They could see the concentration on her face. "The magic feels like it's pulling at my feet," she said, setting off across the room. When she reached the edge of the rug, she crouched down. "Here!" They hurried over and saw Mai's hairslide tangled in the rug's tassels.

"It must have fallen out while I was tickling her," said Ava, untangling the slide. As she handed it to Lily, she noticed two brown leaves lying on the floor, near the window. Where had they come from? The windows had been shut. She went over and picked them up. They were damp as if they'd only recently come in from outside.

Ava frowned. Weird.

"I wish I could wear this crystal all the time," said Sarah.

"Its magic would soon run out," Lily reminded her. When the crystals had been used for too long their magic faded and they had to be recharged.

Sarah nodded. "I should probably take it off before I use the magic up." She pulled the necklace over her head.

Lily glanced at Ava. "You're quiet. Are you OK?"

"Mmm." Ava's fingers curled around the leaves in her hand. She was probably just being silly but even so… "I found these on the floor."

Sarah and Lily looked confused.

"So?" said Lily.

"They're damp, like they've only just come in from outside."

"They were probably caught on Pepper's coat," said Sarah. "She ran over there when we first came in."

"Of course! I'm such a doughnut!" Pepper's coat was long and shaggy and often got tangled with leaves or twigs. Ava shoved the leaves in her pocket and forgot about them as her tummy rumbled and she realized she was starving. "Let's go and get something to eat."

Pepper jumped down from the sofa, stretched and trotted over but as she passed the bottom shelf of curios, the little dog stopped dead. She looked at the shelf and growled.

"Pepper?" said Ava. Pepper hesitated but then shook herself and bounded out through the door.

CHAPTER FIVE

Lily came out of the house with a grumpy-looking Mai the next morning. "I said Mai could walk with us because she didn't want to go to school. I hope that's OK?"

"Sure," said Ava easily.

"It's my spelling test today and I'm tired," Mai sighed. "The monster came back last night."

"I sometimes have nightmares too," Ava told Mai.

"I already said it wasn't a nightmare!" Mai said, frowning.

"All right," said Lily soothingly. "The monster was real but now it's gone and you're fine. Come on, let's get to school. Be careful not to slip on any puddles today!"

But to their surprise all the puddles on the way to school had been smashed.

"Weird!" said Ava.

Lily shrugged. "At least it means we won't slip over." She turned to her sister. "OK, Mai, while we're walking, I'll test you on your spellings."

"I don't want to do my spelling test!" whined Mai.

"I know but you're going to have to so you might as well learn them."

Mai let Lily test her as they walked along the streets, sounding out the words, her breath freezing into icy clouds on the air. Every so often Ava thought she heard a rustle in the hedges as if an animal was following them. Her scalp prickled. She knew it was crazy but she had a feeling they were being watched.

"It's so cold!" said Lily when she'd reached the end of the spellings.

"Freezing," Ava agreed, trying not to think about the rustling noises. "I hope it snows."

"Me too!" said Mai. "Then we can go sledging. I've got a pink sledge," she told Ava proudly. "Daddy bought it for me last year."

Lily squeezed her hand. "But this year you'd better be more careful." She turned to Ava. "Mai fell off her sledge and landed in a bush last time. She hurt her leg."

"I was going really fast," said Mai.

"It sounds fun!" said Ava with a grin.

As they reached the school gates, they saw the

twins, Joe and Isaac, getting out of their dad's car.

Cici walked past them with her mum. "No scooters today?" Cici's mum said to the twins' dad.

"No. Someone took them from our garage in the night," he replied.

Cici's mum looked shocked. "Who'd steal a couple of kids' scooters? That's so unkind."

"I know," said the twins' dad. "Luckily, they didn't take anything else."

"I want my scooter back," said Joe sadly.

"Me too," said Isaac.

Ava felt sorry for them. They might not be very nice at times but they were only five and it was horrible that someone had taken their scooters.

But suddenly there was a distraction. "Snow!" Mai squealed. Ava looked up and saw Mai was right. Fat white flakes of snow were starting to drift down from the heavy sky.

*

By home time, the snow was lying thickly on the ground. The children piled out of school, charging around the playground, throwing snowballs at each other and seeing how far they could slide in the snow while the teachers tried to calm them down. When Mai saw the older girls, she ran over.

"How did you get on with your spelling test?" Ava asked.

"It didn't happen!" Mai said happily. "Mrs Jelson had to go home. Her burglar alarm was going off."

"Did the burglars take anything?" asked Lily in concern.

"No. Mrs Jelson told us it was a false alarm," said Mai. "But it meant we didn't have to do our spellings."

"Result!" said Ava, fist-bumping her and wishing her spelling test had been cancelled too.

Lily and Mai's mum came into the
playground, pushing Huy in his buggy. They
ran over with Mai. "Mummy!" cried Mai,
hugging her.

Her mum smiled and hugged her back. "Brr,
it's cold, isn't it?"

"I'm going to go back to Ava's with Sarah,
Mum," Lily said.

"Are you sure your mum doesn't mind," Cai
said to Ava.

"Mum doesn't mind at all," said Ava

truthfully. Her mum was very easy-going.

"OK, I'll come and pick you up before tea," Cai said to Lily. "Oh, one other thing. I've booked you and Mai places in a theatre class on Saturday afternoons."

"A theatre course?" Lily echoed.

"Yes, it's an hour's singing, an hour's acting and an hour's dancing and you do a show at the end of term."

"Yippee!" said Mai in delight.

"But, Mum," Lily protested. "I don't like acting!"

"Mummy, I really want Lily to come with me," said Mai, tugging at her mum's sleeve.

Cai gave Lily a hopeful look. "Please, Lily, you'll go with Mai, won't you? I'm sure you'll find it fun."

Lily hesitated but then nodded. "All right."

Her mum smiled. "Thanks, love."

Lily and the others set off. "I can't believe I've got to do a theatre class," Lily said despondently.

"I hate being on stage."

"You should have told your mum you didn't want to do it," said Sarah.

Lily sighed. "Then Mai wouldn't go."

"So now you have to do something you hate? That's not fair. Talk to your mum and tell her how you feel," said Sarah.

Lily shook her head. "Mum's really tired at the moment because Huy is being so difficult. I'll just go to this theatre thing. It's easier."

When they reached Fentiman Road, the street where Ava and Lily lived, they saw Emma, Lily's next-door neighbour, knocking on doors.

Seeing them, she waved. "Hi, girls. You haven't seen Marmalade, have you? He hasn't been home since last night."

They shook their heads.

"We'll keep an eye out," Lily promised.

"Thanks," Emma said gratefully. "It's not like him to stay out."

They walked on to Curio House, which was

at the top of the street. Ava pushed open the tall metal gates. The walled garden wrapped around the house and the lawn was blanketed with snow.

"Let's make a snowman!" said Ava.

They dumped their school bags inside and went to get Pepper before racing out into the cold garden again. Their boots sank into the crisp snow. It was perfect for making a snowman with. They rolled snowballs across the grass, making them bigger and bigger until they had a

huge body and a smaller head.

Pepper loved the snow too! She charged around, burying her head and trying to eat it.

When the snowman was built, Ava fetched some walnuts for his eyes and mouth and a carrot for his nose as well as a scarf to wrap around his neck. "No, the carrot's not for you!" she told Pepper as the little dog tried to grab it from her hands. She poked it into place. "There!" she said happily.

"Our snowman's looking SNOW, SNOW good!" said Lily, with a grin.

"I SNOW!" Ava grinned back.

Sarah groaned at their bad jokes. "I'm getting cold. Let's go in."

"Yep, it's hot chocolate time!" said Ava. She called Pepper who was sniffing at the middle Curio Room window again. Ava frowned, feeling like something wasn't right. Her eyes flicked left and right as she looked at the large windows on either side of it. Something was different about the middle one but she couldn't work out what. The panes of glass on all three were frosted up. Icicles hung from the stone lintels above them all…

"Come on, Ava!" called Lily.

Ava gave them one last puzzled look and followed the others inside.

They stripped off their damp gloves and coats. Pepper had little balls of ice caught on her shaggy legs and Ava carefully melted them with lukewarm water while Sarah and Lily heated up three mugs of milk so they could all have hot chocolate.

Towelling Pepper's legs dry, Ava couldn't stop thinking about the window. She had a very strong feeling that something hadn't been quite right. Just like the feeling she'd had when she'd found the leaves on the floor and when she'd heard rustling in the hedges as they walked to school.

"I think something magic might be going on!" she burst out.

Sarah and Lily, who were in the middle of making the hot chocolate, turned round in surprise. "What?" said Lily, spilling a spoonful of powder on the floor. "Why?"

"It's just one of my feelings," said Ava. "I want to check the curios again."

They took their mugs of hot chocolate through to the Curio Room. Ava studied the shelves but just like the day before, all the curios seemed to be where they should be.

"What makes you think something magic's going on?" Sarah asked Ava.

She told them about Pepper barking, the rustling in the hedges and her feeling that something about one of the windows was wrong. "There were the leaves I found too," she said. "I know it's not much to go on and I can't explain it... I just feel like I'm right. I wish there was a way to find out for sure."

"A way to understand what's going on," said Sarah slowly. Her eyes widened and she ran to the desk and grabbed the box of crystals. "The Jade Crystal!" She opened the lid and read out: "*Jade. The Dream Crystal. Jade enables dreams to bring insight and understanding. It also promotes sleep.*" She looked up excitedly. "Why don't you try sleeping with the Jade Crystal tonight, Ava?"

Ava felt excitement flare through her. "That's an awesome idea! I will!"

CHAPTER SIX

Ava was so keen to go to bed that night that she ate her tea super fast. "Whoa! What's the rush?" Fran said as Ava leaped up to put her plate in the dishwasher. She indicated her own half-eaten plate of lasagne. "I'm still eating."

"Sorry, Mum," said Ava, sitting back down. "I'm just tired and I want to go to bed early."

"Busy day?" her mum said.

"Yep." Ava hid her smile. If only her mum knew!

"This half term has gone really fast," Fran

said. "I'm glad you've settled in and made friends. Lily and Sarah are great. Which reminds me, I spoke to Cai earlier and asked if you can stay at her house tomorrow night. Auntie Abi has managed to get two tickets to a show in London and I'm going to stay the night with her."

"That's fine," said Ava. Auntie Abi was her godmother. "It'll be fun staying at Lily's. But what about Pepper?"

"Cai said she can stay too if you keep her up in Lily's room and away from Huy as much as you can. She's inviting Sarah as well." Fran chuckled. "I imagine you might have Mai joining you too."

"She wants to be with us all the time!"

"Maybe Lily should tell her that you sometimes want to be on your own," said Fran.

"She won't. She doesn't want to upset Mai – or her mum." Ava shook her head. "She's even having to go to a theatre class on Saturdays now.

She really doesn't want to go but Mai won't go without her."

Her mum sighed. "Poor Lily. It's lovely she's so caring and responsible but she shouldn't always have to do what her little sister wants. Why don't you suggest she talks to her mum about it?"

"Sarah tried," said Ava. "But Lily won't."

"But if she doesn't tell her mum how she's feeling, her mum will never know. Maybe you should talk to her again about it, sweetie."

"OK," said Ava.

Her mum got up and kissed her on the head.

They cleared up then Ava went upstairs with Pepper. She had the quickest shower ever and then took the necklace and the Jade Crystal out of the box. Putting the necklace on, she held the Jade in her hands, feeling its long and slow vibrations throbbing through her fingers. Ava yawned, feeling a wave of tiredness sweep over her. She fitted the crystal into the necklace. It didn't sparkle brightly in the same way as some of the other crystals. Instead it gave off a soft green glow, like a comforting night light. She tucked the necklace inside her pyjama top then turned her bedside light off and snuggled under the duvet. Pepper stretched out at the end of Ava's bed, turning on her back and sticking one leg straight up in the air.

"Night, Peps," Ava murmured. A few seconds later, she was fast asleep.

*

In her dreams, Ava saw a jumble of images: she was flying like a bird, swooping high above the town, and she could feel her powerful wings beating and the frosty air against her face as she flew over a street lined with houses and trees. *My street*, Ava realized. The dream changed and she was flying upwards in a wood, past trees that were bare of leaves and bursting out into the starry sky, a feeling of satisfaction radiating through her. Then she was back above town, swooping towards a house that looked familiar. She landed on the windowsill of one of the upper windows and pressed her clawed hands against the glass...

Ava woke and sat up. Glancing at her alarm clock she saw that it was 5 a.m. The images she had seen didn't make any sense. Why was she dreaming about being a bird? She pulled the crystal out from under her pyjama top. It was still glowing softly.

Why's it not telling me what I need to know?

But even as the thought formed, Ava knew the answer. She hadn't focused on what she wanted it to reveal to her before she'd gone to sleep, she'd just let the crystal do its own thing.

Pepper was snoring softly at the end of her bed and it was still pitch-black outside.

I'll try again, Ava decided. She lay back down, holding the pendant in her hand and concentrating on what she wanted to know. *Has any magic escaped? Is one of the curios causing trouble?*

She felt sleep overwhelming her and this time she saw Mai in the Curio Room on the day they'd been playing hide-and-seek, but as she looked at the little girl, she realized she seemed to be watching her from a strange viewpoint. *It's almost like I'm sitting with the curios*, she thought as she watched Mai picking something off the bottom shelf... Next, she was flying again before landing beside a frozen puddle, and for a moment she saw a strange reflection in the frozen ice. Was there a lump on her head? But before she could look more clearly, she had smashed the ice with her fist and taken off again...

Images continued to stream through her head: she scaled the wall of a house, reaching for a box with a blinking light ... pulled open a garage door and hauled out two scooters ... grabbed a ginger cat and flew away with it ... opened a shed that looked familiar and darted inside... Finally, she saw her house from the back garden. She flew down and landed on the

ledge of the middle Curio Room window. She
pulled it up but as she did so, she caught sight of
her reflection in the glass – a grey face, bulging
eyes, a lumpy horn and an open mouth.

She woke with a start and sat bolt upright.

"Pepper! It's the gargoyle who's doing all these
things! It's come to life!"

Pepper leaped up as Ava threw back the
covers. Her alarm clock now said 6:01. Ava
pulled the necklace off and put it on her bedside
table. The heating hadn't come on yet and the
early-morning air was icy cold. She grabbed her
dressing gown and, shoving her arms inside, ran
quietly downstairs with Pepper beside her.

Ava didn't have a clue why the gargoyle was
doing the things she had seen, what had woken
up its magic or what kind of magic she was
dealing with, she just knew she had to stop it
before someone saw it flying around outside.

She rushed into the Curio Room and ran
to the shelves. Skidding to a halt, she stared at

them in horror. The space where the gargoyle should've been was empty. It had gone!

"Woof! Woof! Woof!" Pepper barked furiously, racing across the room.

Ava's gaze flew to what Pepper was barking at. The gargoyle was there, crouching on the seat, its hands on the sash window! As Pepper charged towards it, it pulled the window up. An icy blast of air buffeted in as its bat-like wings unfurled behind it. It hissed at Pepper like an angry cat, its mouth opening wide, then it leaped outside and with two strong flaps of its leathery wings flew upwards.

Ava felt as if all the air had been punched out of her.

"No!" she gasped, running forwards and looking out. The gargoyle was beside an upstairs window. It landed on the ledge and pulled it open, hopping inside. What was it doing? Then Ava realized something. That was HER bedroom!

She turned and charged back out of the room and up the stairs. Panting, she flung herself into her room. She was just in time to see the gargoyle take the Jade Crystal from the necklace with its long, clawed fingers and then leap out of the window again.

"Oh, pants!" she whispered in horror as it swooped away across the night sky.

CHAPTER SEVEN

"What do you mean – the stone gargoyle's flown away?" Lily's voice had been groggy with sleep when she had answered the phone a few seconds ago but now she sounded thoroughly awake – and extremely alarmed. Ava had FaceTimed her and she could see her sitting in bed, her hair sticking up. "What are you talking about, Ava? What's going on?"

Ava gabbled out what had happened, telling her about her dreams and the gargoyle jumping out of the Curio Room. "It flew to my room, grabbed the Jade Crystal and zoomed off into the night!" she finished.

"But where's it gone?" Lily said in dismay.

"I don't know." Ava's mouth felt as dry as sandpaper. What if someone else saw it and discovered that the curios were magic? What if it did something dreadful?

"I'm going out to try and find it…"

"Wait! You can't go rushing off on your own in the dark," said Lily. "Come round to my house at eight o'clock. I'll phone Sarah and we can try to think up a plan."

Ava reluctantly agreed. "OK." She paced around her room, watching the minutes slowly tick by. She wanted to go to Lily's house right there and then but she knew Lily's mum would ask too many questions if she appeared quite so early in the morning.

Her thoughts raced as she walked up and down. She knew now why she'd had a feeling something was different about the middle window the other day – there had been no snow on the ledge because the gargoyle had knocked it off when it had been going in and out, and the leaves she had found must have been brought in on its clawed feet. But how long had it been awake and what kind of magic were they dealing with?

Opening her bedside drawer, Ava took out the notebook that had belonged to Great-Aunt Enid. The old lady had written notes about the curios and crystals but her handwriting was hard to read and the notes were very jumbled up. Ava leafed through the pages, wishing that she didn't find reading so hard. She found a page with the word '*Gargoyle*' at the top. She tried to make out what the words said. She could manage the first few: "*The Gargoyle is a…*"

She paused. "*Gu—? Gua—?*" She tried to sound out the word but it was too hard. She shut the notebook in frustration. Hopefully Lily would be able to read it.

We've got to get the gargoyle back. The thought beat through her as she pushed her hands through her thick hair. *But how?*

*

Ava arrived at Lily's house with Pepper dead on eight o'clock. As she turned up the driveway, Emma from next door came out of her house. Marmalade, the big ginger cat, was with her. He glared at Pepper as she bounded towards him.

"You found him!" Ava said to Emma. She'd been sure that in one of her dreams she had seen the gargoyle picking Marmalade up and she'd been worrying about what it had done with him.

Emma smiled. "Yes. A lady found him miles
and miles away – near Biddleston Wood. I
don't know how he got there. Luckily, he's
microchipped and when she took him to her
vet's they were able to find out he belonged to
me." She bent down to stroke the big cat who
purred happily. "I'm so glad he's back."

"Me too," said Ava in relief.

Ava hurried to Lily's door but just as she
reached it, Lily's dad came out carrying a

89

swimming float and towel. Mai was following him. "I don't want to go swimming, Daddy! I don't like putting my head in the water. It makes me feel like I'm drowning."

"You've got to learn to swim, Mai," said her dad, unlocking the car. "Now please tell me where your bag of swimming things has gone."

"I told you. The monster has it," said Mai.

Her dad took a breath, as if he was trying very hard to be patient, and then he spotted Ava. "Hello, Ava." Mai ran over to give Ava a hug. "You're here bright and early. Lily's in the kitchen."

"Thanks," said Ava.

"Come on, in the car, Mai," said her dad, opening the car door for her. "I'll buy you a new swimsuit at the leisure centre. Your old one was getting too small anyway."

"I don't WANT to!" Mai stomped into the car and flung herself into her seat just as Sarah arrived. She and Ava went inside.

A few minutes later, they were all sitting in Lily's bedroom. Sarah had a notebook and a pen poised. "So let's get this straight. At some point the gargoyle has come to life and it's been coming and going from the Curio Room."

Ava nodded. "It's always been on the shelf when we've looked so that's why we didn't notice."

"But why did it take the Jade Crystal and what's it been doing when it's outside?" said Sarah.

"I think it's been following us for some of the time," said Ava remembering the rustling she'd heard in the hedges. She tried to remember what she had seen in her dreams that night. "It smashed the puddles and took the twins' scooters. I saw it flying out of a wood and climbing up the wall of a house towards a box. Oh, and I saw it sitting on a window ledge – my window I guess." She shivered at the memory. "It must have been spying on me for some reason."

She remembered something else. "I also saw it picking up Marmalade."

"Marmalade?" Lily said in alarm.

"He's OK." Ava quickly told them what she'd found out from Emma. "He was found near a wood and I saw the gargoyle flying away from a wood, so I think the gargoyle put him there."

Sarah had been writing everything down. Now she stopped. "But why would the gargoyle put Marmalade in a wood?"

Ava shrugged. "He doesn't like cats?"

Lily and Sarah's eyebrows rose high enough to hit their hairlines. Ava looked at them helplessly. "Well, have either of you got a better explanation?"

"No," said Sarah. "All the things it's been doing seem completely random to me."

Ava felt like there was something they weren't seeing – a link that would make everything suddenly make sense. "There's got to be a reason why it's doing all these things.

Maybe the notebook will help. I found a page with some notes on the gargoyle but I couldn't read it." She pulled the notebook out of her bag and handed it to Lily. She'd marked the page she'd found with a bookmark made from a torn-off piece of paper.

Lily poured over the page. She could read faster than anyone Ava knew. "OK, it says here that the gargoyle came from a church roof."

"Yes, a church in Eastwold," Sarah put in. "It said that on the gargoyle's label. It was made around the mid 1200s."

1200s. A memory tugged at Ava's brain. When had she been talking about the 1200s recently?

"Does the notebook say anything else?" Sarah asked.

"That it's a guardian gargoyle, whatever that means," said Lily. "It also says: *Extreme urge to protect. Treat with caution if the magic spirit is awake. Beware the claws and teeth.*"

Ava shivered. "That doesn't sound good."

Sarah checked her phone. "I'm going to have to go to gymnastics in a minute."

"And Mum and I are supposed to be going into town to buy some Christmas presents," Ava remembered. "Shall we meet at lunchtime?"

"I can't. I've got this theatre thing with Mai," said Lily. "I really don't want to go."

"You should say something," said Ava, remembering the conversation she'd had with her mum, but Lily just shook her head.

"Don't forget we're having a sleepover tonight.

If you bring the crystals, Ava, we can try and work out a proper plan for how to catch the gargoyle, then," said Sarah, getting up and reaching for her coat.

"Yep!" said Ava. Despite her worry, her mouth twitched with a smile. "Our plan will ROCK!"

Lily giggled. "We'll leave no STONE unturned as we try to find it."

Sarah rolled her eyes at them. "This is serious, you two. It's a pity we used all the seeds of the afypnistis flower when we were trying to attract the nature spirit. We could have used them to catch the gargoyle. I guess we'll have to think of something else. What do you think gargoyles like?"

"Churches? Tall buildings? Stone?" suggested Lily.

"B-ROCK-oli?" said Ava.

Sarah shot her an exasperated look.

*

Ava said goodbye to the others and set off home. As she walked along the snowy pavement, something that Sarah had said played in her mind. *The afypnistis flower.* They'd used it in their last adventure. Its seeds and flowers could attract spirits and awaken them…

That's it! The realization shot through her. Her dreams had shown her Mai in the Curio Room, picking something up off the shelf. She replayed the memory in her mind's eye and saw Mai pushing a stray white petal into the gargoyle's open mouth. A stray white petal that must have been left over from when the afypnistis flower had bloomed. Of course! That's what had woken the gargoyle up!

And now it could be anywhere, doing anything, she thought, a chill running down her spine. What if they never found it? Or what if someone else found it first? *We can't let that happen*, she realized. *We have to find it – and fast!*

CHAPTER EIGHT

It snowed again that afternoon. Ava's mum helped Ava carry her and Pepper's things round to Lily's for the sleepover. They reached Lily's house just as she arrived back from the theatre class with her mum and Mai. Lily got out of the car looking miserable.

"How was it?" Ava said.

"Awful!" Lily whispered so her mum couldn't hear. "I hated it!"

Cai undid Mai's seat belt and Mai ran around the car to Ava. "The theatre class was brilliant!

Cici was there. We did singing and dancing and acting." She spun round. "We're all going to be in a play!"

Ava glanced at Lily.

"Thanks for having Ava and Pepper tonight," Fran said to Cai.

"It's no problem," said Cai, carrying Huy over. "Richard and I need to go out for a few hours but our usual babysitter is coming round – Jasmine. She's lovely. I'm sure Ava and Sarah will like her."

"Jasmine's nice!" said Mai. She turned to Ava. "She'll play games with us tonight."

"No, *you* can play with Jasmine tonight, Mai," said Lily sharply. "Ava, me and Sarah are doing stuff on our own."

Mai looked taken aback.

Cai gave her older daughter a swift look. "Are you OK, Lily?"

"Yes," Lily muttered.

"Are you sure?" said Cai.

"I'm fine!" Lily snapped, and stomped inside.

"Goodness," Cai said to Fran. "I don't know what's the matter with her. She's been in a bad mood ever since I picked her up."

Ava and her mum exchanged looks. "Why don't you go after Lily, sweetie, and check she's OK? I'll see you tomorrow. Have a good sleepover."

Ava gave her a hug. "OK. Bye, Mum. Enjoy the theatre!"

She hurried after Lily with Pepper.

"Why was Lily cross, Mummy?" she heard Mai saying as she went into the house.

"I don't know, love," said Cai, sounding puzzled.

Ava ran up the stairs with Pepper and found Lily in her bedroom, sitting on her bed. Her arms were folded and her expression was unhappy.

"Are you OK?" Ava asked her.

"Yes," Lily muttered. "I'm just fed up with always having to do what Mai wants and having

her with us all the time."
Pepper jumped up on the
bed and started to lick
her ear.

"Sorry!" Ava said,
trying to pull her
off.

Lily smiled and
cuddled Pepper.
"It's OK, I don't
mind."

"Maybe if you talk to
your mum…" Ava began.

"No," Lily quickly said.

There was a light knock at her door and Cai
looked in. "Is everything all right, Lily?"

Ava willed Lily to say something but Lily
just forced a smile. "Yes," she said. "I'm sorry I
snapped."

"Don't worry," her mum said. "I just wanted to
check you were OK. Do you want to go sledging

when Sarah gets here? If you do, Dad said he'll take you out while I give Mai and Huy their tea."

"We'll get the sledges!" said Lily.

She and Ava went downstairs with Pepper.

"You should have said something to her," Ava said.

Lily shook her head.

They went out the back door into the garden where the shed was. As they approached it, a memory felt like it was trying to swim up in Ava's brain. She frowned.

Lily opened the door. "The sledges!" she exclaimed. The three sledges all had big holes that looked as if they had been smashed with a rock. Bits of bright plastic littered the floor of the packed shed.

Ava suddenly realized why it had seemed so familiar. "I saw this shed in my dream! I bet the gargoyle did this!"

Lily stared at her open-mouthed. "But why?"

Ava was mystified.

They went to tell her mum and dad about the sledges. They were both astonished. "Who'd break three sledges?" said Lily's dad.

"I've no idea," said Cai. "But there are some strange things going on at the moment. Cici's mum told me the twins had their scooters stolen and I bumped into Mrs Jelson when I was in town and she told me someone had tampered with her burglar alarm the other day. She had to leave school to go and sort it out."

Ava's scalp prickled. The burglar alarm!

Could that be the box on the wall of the house with a blinking light that she'd seen the gargoyle climbing up to?

As soon as Sarah arrived, Ava told her and Lily about the alarm and Sarah added both that and the damaged sledges to her list of things the gargoyle had done.

"So it smashed the puddles, stole the scooters, took Marmalade, made Mrs Jelson's alarm go off, broke the sledges in the shed, sat outside Ava's window and took the Jade Crystal," said Sarah, reading out the list.

"And they're just the things we know about," Lily said. "It may have done other things too."

Ava rubbed her head. All of these things had to be connected, but she just couldn't work out how.

*

After tea Jasmine arrived and Mai wanted all of them to play games in the lounge.

Ava could sense Lily's frustration growing.

"We'll be able to talk as soon as Mai's in bed," she whispered to her.

At quarter past seven, Jasmine took Mai upstairs to read her a story.

"Phew!" said Lily as they went into her bedroom and sat down on her bed.

"Time to plan!" said Sarah, taking out her notebook. "Who's had any good ideas?"

They all looked hopefully at each other but no one spoke.

By the time they heard Jasmine leave Mai's room, they still hadn't come up with a plan.

Jasmine tapped on the door. "Are you lot OK?" she asked.

"We're fine, thanks," said Lily.

"Cool. I'm going to go downstairs and do some schoolwork. Come and find me if you need anything," Jasmine said. She went downstairs, humming.

Ava took the crystals out. "Maybe the Amethyst can help. It brings you things you want, remember?"

Sarah looked doubtful. "But what if it brings us another gargoyle? We definitely don't want two of them!"

"No way," said Lily. "Though I think using the crystals is a good idea."

"How about the Obsidian?" said Sarah. "It helps you see things that are elsewhere…" She broke off as Mai came in. Ava quickly slid the box of crystals under her legs to hide it.

"Can I sleep in here?" Mai asked Lily.

Lily tensed. "Not tonight. Go back to your own room."

"But the monster might get me," whined Mai.

Lily let out a frustrated exclamation. "Mai! The monster isn't real. How many times do I have to tell you that?"

"It is real," Mai said stubbornly. "It sits on my windowsill and watches me every night."

Something went click in Ava's brain. They'd been thinking the gargoyle was sitting on her windowsill but maybe it had been sitting on Mai's!

"I want to stay in here," said Mai.

Lily lost her temper and jumped to her feet. "No! Get out, Mai. Out! Out! Out!" She pushed her sister towards the door.

Mai tripped over Ava's sleeping bag and fell with a squeal.

"Ow! You're mean!" she cried. "You hurt me…" She broke off as Lily's window opened. "The monster!" she shrieked, pointing behind them.

They all swung round. The stone gargoyle was perched on the window ledge! Pepper let out a volley of loud barks as the freezing night air rushed in. The gargoyle swooped at Mai and grabbed her with its clawed hands. The little girl screamed and struggled but the gargoyle scooped her up and sprang back on to the window ledge. With a flap of its powerful wings, it jumped into the night and carried her away!

CHAPTER NINE

Ava rushed to the window with Lily and Sarah. "Mai!" The shriek tore out of Lily.

"What are we going to do?" gasped Sarah as the gargoyle flew away with Mai clutched in its arms. It wasn't very big but it was clearly very strong.

Ava felt as if the pieces of the jigsaw had just fitted together in her mind but she didn't have time to think about it. Mai was in danger and they needed to do something! She grabbed the Bloodstone, feeling energy and power surge through her. Picking up the necklace, she pushed the Bloodstone into the pendant and pulled it over her head as the crystal began to sparkle like a star. "I'm going after her!"

"Wait!" she heard Sarah shout. Pepper barked as she ran downstairs and past the lounge where Jasmine was deep in study. But Ava didn't stop. She raced out the front door. She could just see the shadowy winged shape in the sky. Her heart hammered as she started to run down the street after it, the magic helping her run faster than she would ever normally be able to.

Mai's the missing link – she connects everything.
The thought beat through Ava as she ran. She could see it now. The gargoyle had been sitting by Mai's window, the sledges belonged to Mai's family, Marmalade belonged to her neighbour, the missing scooters belonged to the twins in her class, the alarm that had been damaged belonged to her teacher. Even the puddles had been smashed after she had slid on them. Ava still didn't have a clue why the gargoyle had done those things, she just knew now that they all connected back to Mai. But why had it snatched her? Where was it taking her? Her stomach twisted into knots. What was it planning on doing with her?

Ava skidded round a corner, her trainers – now soaked – throwing up a mini wave of slush. Her eyes were fixed on the gargoyle ahead of her in the sky. Mai was completely still in its arms. A wave of fear engulfed her. Why wasn't the little girl moving or calling out? The winged creature swooped lower. Was it planning on landing? Ava drew in a breath of freezing air as she saw it land on the turrets of the old stone folly – the little tower she and Lily passed on their way to school.

As Ava charged up to the tower, the gargoyle opened its mouth with a fierce hiss. The claws on its feet gripping the stones looked like knives and its eyes burned menacingly as it clutched Mai to its chest.

"Give … Mai … back!" Ava panted furiously.

But to her horror, the gargoyle folded its wings tight against its back and leaped into the hollow tower!

"No!" Ava cried. She charged up to the building, grabbing hold of the iron bars that blocked the entrance. The cold of the metal bit into her hands as she peered between them, into the shadowy interior. The gargoyle landed safely and carried Mai down a flight of old stone steps. Ava's heart pounded. It was taking Mai into the maze of tunnels that ran underneath the town!

"Come back! Stop!" she shouted but it had vanished from sight.

Hearing a bark, she swung round. Lily, Sarah and Pepper were racing towards her.

"Ava!" Lily exclaimed, looking around frantically. "Where's Mai?"

"It's taken her into the tunnels!" Ava gabbled out what had happened.

Lily looked distraught. "We have to get her back before it hurts her."

If it hasn't hurt her already, Ava thought worriedly.

"We need to get into the tunnels and follow it," said Lily.

Ava looked at the tower. Maybe with the extra energy and strength from the Bloodstone, she could climb up it but she wouldn't be able to jump down inside like the gargoyle. Even with the magic she'd break an arm or leg or worse. "If we got a rope, maybe I could climb down the inside of the tower and…"

"No, we all need to go. You can't do this on your own. Are there other entrances to the tunnels, Lily?" Sarah said.

"Yes, in some of the oldest buildings in town," said Lily. "But we can't break into people's houses…"

"We might not need to!" Sarah turned to Ava. "Ava, the other day your mum told Cai that parts of your house are really old and that you have a cellar?"

Ava suddenly understood. "You think there might be an entrance to the tunnels from our cellar?"

"It's worth a try," said Sarah.

"But how can we get in?" said Lily. "Ava's mum's away."

Ava's face lit up with an idea. "I think I know a way in! Come on!"

*

They ran to Curio House with Pepper bounding along beside them. Ava pulled off the necklace and put it in her coat pocket. If the crystals were used for too long their energy ran out. They could be recharged with the Selenite Wand that came with the crystals but it took a while.

"Did you bring the other crystals with you?" Ava panted as they ran.

Sarah patted the strap of her backpack. "Yes, and the notebook too. We also left a note for Jasmine. We're lucky she was so into her studying that she didn't hear anything. Imagine if she'd come up and seen the gargoyle! We told her not to worry and that we'd be back soon."

Ava felt a shiver run down her spine. Would they be back soon? She had no idea.

They reached her house. "If the gargoyle can get in through the window then so can we!" she said, leading the way across the garden, the snow crunching under her feet. She grabbed hold of the bottom of the sash window and pulled it up. It rattled and creaked stiffly, moving a few centimetres. The others helped her and they managed to open it just wide enough for them all to climb through. The Curio Room was silent and still as they landed on the rug. The only light came from the pale round disc of the moon in the sky, casting shadows across the floor. The air in the room was tense. Ava shivered. It felt like all the curios were watching them.

"Come on," she whispered even though there was no one in the house.

In the kitchen, Ava turned on the light and they all looked towards the flight of three stone steps leading down to a corridor that led to a small wooden door. Heart beating fast, Ava went down the steps and twisted the metal knob. The door swung open and they peered into the gloom. All they could see were more stone steps.

"Is there a light?" Sarah asked.

"There are some torches in the cupboard over there," said Ava. But then she spotted a switch on the wall of the cellar. She flicked it on and a single lightbulb flickered. It didn't cast very much light but it was enough for them to see that there were empty shelves lining the stone walls as well as piles of wooden packing crates and mounds of tarpaulin. Thick white ropes of cobwebs hung from the ceiling.

Ava glanced at Lily. She knew she hated spiders. "Wait here. I'll see if I can find an entrance."

"No." Lily gulped. "It'll be quicker if we all search." She went down the steps, gasping as a cobweb brushed her hair.

Ava followed, Pepper sticking close beside her, but when she reached the bottom of the steps she realized Sarah wasn't behind her. "Sarah?"

Sarah appeared in the cellar entrance with three torches in her hands. "I thought these might be a good idea."

She handed one torch to Ava and the other to Lily. They swung the beams around the cellar walls. Mould blackened the stones and the air felt damp. *Please let there be a door*, Ava thought.

"There!" said Lily suddenly, pointing to the floor in one corner where there was an outline of a trapdoor, half covered by some mouldy tarpaulins. Lily pulled the tarpaulins to one side, revealing a metal ring. She hauled at it. "Help me!" she gasped.

Ava and Sarah joined her. The trapdoor was heavy but they heaved it open. It crashed back on to the cellar floor.

Shining their torches into the darkness below, they saw stone steps leading further underground.

Before Ava could even take a step, Lily had pushed past her, her torch cutting a narrow path of light through the inky black. "Mai's down here somewhere!" she called urgently. "Come on!"

CHAPTER TEN

The stone walls of the tunnels were damp
and at times the roof was so low they had to
duck underneath it to be able to keep moving
forward. The air was freezing cold and the
darkness felt suffocating. It seemed to press in
around them, stealing the breath from their
lungs.

Pepper stayed close to Ava's side, her tail low,
her brown eyes worried. The beams of light
from the torches were not strong enough to do
much more than light the way directly in front

of the girls' feet.

"It's very creepy in here," Sarah said uneasily.

Ava nodded. Her senses felt like they were on red alert, waiting for something to jump out of the shadows at any moment. She remembered Lily telling her that people had died in the tunnels.

Ghosts don't exist, she told herself firmly.

But what about zombies or vampires or werewolves…

She quickly squashed the thought.

"Poor Mai's going to be terrified," said Lily anxiously. "Why do you think the gargoyle brought her down here?"

Neither Ava nor Sarah answered. Ava wondered if Sarah was thinking the same as her – that whatever the gargoyle's reason, it couldn't be good.

The tunnel opened out into a mini cave. Two other tunnels led out of it. "Which way now?" said Lily.

For a
moment they all
stood there uncertainly and
then Sarah exclaimed, "I know!" She
took out the box of crystals and removed the
Lapis Lazuli. "Let's use this."

"Good idea!" said Ava. She took the necklace
out of her pocket and removed the Bloodstone.
"Put it in this so it's at full power."

· The crystal had already begun to glow in
Sarah's hand. As she fitted it into the pendant,

the glow became a sparkle. It lit up the darkness with its clear blue light and Ava felt her fear slightly fade.

"This tunnel," Sarah said decisively, heading into the right-hand tunnel. "I can feel the crystal pulling me this way."

Ava and LiIy followed her. With the light from the crystal adding to the light from their torches they could see much better and they broke into a run, jumping over rocks that littered the floor until they came out in another cave. This one was bigger, with four tunnels, some big boulders and stalactites – pointed rock formations hanging down from the ceiling that looked like stone icicles.

"Which way now, Sarah?" said Lily.

Sarah turned slowly round, looking at each tunnel. "I don't know. The magic's suddenly not feeling as clear."

Ava felt a spider-tingle of worry creep down her spine. "What do you mean?"

"I can't seem to sense which tunnel to take. Be quiet, both of you, let me concentrate." Ava and Lily waited anxiously as Sarah shut her eyes and focused on the crystal. The silence stretched out. Ava noticed that the crystal seemed to be shining less brightly but before she could say anything she heard a voice in one of the tunnels.

Her heart almost jumped out of her chest. "Who's that?" she whispered.

"What?" said Lily.

Ava heard the voice again and then footsteps. Whoever it was, was coming towards them! "Quick! Hide!" she gasped, grabbing Lily and Sarah's arms and pulling them behind a nearby boulder. Pepper bounded with them. "Shhh!" Ava hissed.

"Why are we hiding?" whispered Sarah.

"Didn't you hear the voice and footsteps?" Ava breathed.

Sarah shook her head.

"I didn't hear anything either," whispered Lily.

Ava put her fingers to her lips and listened hard. In the silence she heard the footsteps again. They were getting closer and closer, they sounded like they were almost in the cave. Maybe it was the gargoyle. A feeling of dread swept over her. She put a hand over Pepper's nose just in case she barked and waited … and waited … and waited.

Nothing happened apart from the cave suddenly seeming to get slightly darker.

She saw Sarah and Lily swapping confused looks.

"I can't hear anything, Ava," whispered Sarah.

Ava suddenly realized that she couldn't either. What had just happened? She was sure someone had been coming into the cave. "I heard a voice and footsteps," she said. "They were coming this way."

Sarah's face relaxed. "Oh, it was just cave ghosts."

"Ghosts?" squeaked Lily.

"Real ghosts?" breathed Ava.

To her astonishment, Sarah smiled. "They're not actual ghosts, don't worry. They're tricks of the mind. I've been caving with my dad and sometimes when you're in a cave and it's really, really quiet, you feel sure you hear voices and footsteps. They sound real but it's a just a phenomenon. Dad calls them cave ghosts."

Ava felt a rush of relief. "Sorry. It really did sound like someone was coming," she said, releasing Pepper who shook herself and trotted out from behind the boulder.

"Better to be safe than sorry," said Sarah. "It could have been the gargoyle."

"Or something else," said Lily with a shudder. "OK, so which way now, Sarah?"

Ava's heart plummeted as she suddenly realized exactly why the cave had seemed to get darker. "Sarah! The Lapis Lazuli! Its magic has run out!"

They all stared at the necklace. The blue stone was no longer sparkling.

"We can recharge it with the Selenite Wand," said Lily.

"It won't work," said Sarah. "The Selenite Wand needs natural light when it's recharging a crystal – preferably moonlight."

Lily looked at the others in dismay. "So what are we going to do? How can we find Mai now?"

"I don't know," said Sarah, swallowing.

"Woof!"

Ava turned and saw Pepper standing in the entrance to one of the tunnels. Her ears were pricked and she was sniffing at the air. "Pepper?"

Putting her nose to the ground, Pepper sniffed around the floor and headed deeper into the tunnel.

"Pepper! Come back!" called Lily.

"No," Ava said suddenly. She knew now that she should have taken more notice of Pepper when she was barking at the window. She must have picked up the scent of the gargoyle after it had started letting itself in and out of the Curio Room. There was no way she was going to make the same mistake again. "Maybe she's smelled the gargoyle!"

"She's smelled something," said Sarah as Pepper trotted down the tunnel, her nose glued to the floor.

Ava and Lily followed her. Looking round, Ava saw Sarah crouching down at the tunnel entrance. "Come on, Sarah!"

"Coming!" Sarah called, running to join them.

They jogged down the tunnel as it twisted and turned. They came to another cave with three tunnels. Pepper didn't hesitate. She bounded down the one that led east. Once again, Sarah paused by the tunnel entrance.

"What are you doing?" Ava asked her.

"I'll explain later," said Sarah, catching them up as they ran round a corner. "No time now. Do you really think Pepper is leading us to the gargoyle?"

"Woof!"

Pepper skidded to a halt and the girls almost ran into her.

"Woof! Woof! Woof!"

Ava felt her stomach drop. "I think she is," she gulped.

They'd reached another small cave and in the middle of it Mai was lying on the floor. The gargoyle was crouched over her, its clawed hand touching her head. Seeing the girls, it glared at them, its eyes charged with menace, and then it flexed its blade-like talons.

Sarah gulped. "OK, what do we do now?"

CHAPTER ELEVEN

"Mai!" Lily yelled, charging forward and throwing herself at the gargoyle.

The gargoyle instantly sprang at her. Its hands slammed into her shoulders, flinging her back on to the hard ground.

"Ow!" Lily cried. The fall had winded her and her words came out in gasps as she tried to draw air into her lungs. "Why's … Mai … not … moving?"

Pepper jumped at the gargoyle, barking furiously. The gargoyle hissed at her. Ava hastily

grabbed Pepper and pulled her back. The last
thing she wanted was for her to become a
gargoyle snack! "Here, Sarah. Hold her!"

"Why? What are you going to do?" Sarah
said, taking hold of Pepper's collar.

Ava pulled the Bloodstone out of her pocket.
As she gripped it, she felt its magic surge into
her. Even without the pendant, she could feel
her body filling with energy. She threw herself
into a spin, turning faster than she would ever
normally be able to do and lashed out with her
foot. It cracked into
the gargoyle's
shoulder.

"Ouch!" she gasped, hopping backwards. It had been like kicking a stone wall and the gargoyle didn't seem to have felt it at all. It reared up angrily, its wings stretching out as Ava bravely attacked again, this time with her fists. But the gargoyle dodged her punches easily. As she turned to try to kick again, it grabbed her foot and tossed her across the cave as easily as if she was a doll. Ava thumped down on to the floor, desperation flooding through her. How could she fight something that didn't feel pain? She gritted her teeth and jumped to her feet again. She didn't know but she was going to try!

Just then a stone whizzed across the cave and bounced off the gargoyle's head on to Mai's leg. "Leave my friends alone!" shouted Sarah, picking up another stone and chucking that at the gargoyle. Her aim was good and it hit the gargoyle's horn. It bounced off and would have landed on Mai too but the gargoyle caught it and chucked it away. It clattered across the floor.

The gargoyle hissed at Sarah
and then it turned to Mai,
its wings forming an
umbrella over her
body.

Ava saw her
opportunity
to get a blow
in while it was
distracted. She
jumped to her feet.

"No, Ava!" Lily
cried. "Leave it alone. You too,
Sarah!"

They both looked at her in surprise.

"We've got things wrong. Look at how gentle
it's being." They looked at the gargoyle and saw
that it was stroking Mai's leg where the stone had
hit her. "I don't think it wants to hurt Mai," Lily
said slowly. "I think it wants to look after her."

The final pieces of the puzzle slotted together

in Ava's brain.

"Of course!" she gasped. "Mai woke it up and now it wants to protect her. It's a *guardian* gargoyle, remember? It smashed the puddles so she wouldn't slip, it took the scooters so the twins wouldn't run into her, it removed Marmalade so he couldn't scratch her..."

"And damaged the sledges so she couldn't hurt herself again!" exclaimed Lily.

"It even set Mrs Jelson's alarm off so she didn't have to do the spelling test she was dreading and took her swimming costume so she didn't have to go swimming," said Ava.

"It's been looking after her," said Lily.

"But why's Mai so still?" said Sarah.

"The Jade Crystal." Now she was looking properly, Ava could see a faint green glow between Mai's fingers. "The gargoyle must have used it to send her to sleep. It was watching at the window and when it saw you push her..."

"It jumped in to protect her," Lily realized.

She looked at the gargoyle crouching protectively over her sister. "But why did it bring her down here?"

"To keep her safe," said Sarah suddenly. "The gargoyle is from the 1200s and that's when the tunnels were built too. I bet it thinks of these tunnels as a place of safety."

They all looked at the gargoyle. It was watching them warily.

"How are we going to get it to give her back?" said Ava.

"Can I have the necklace and the crystals?" said Lily quickly. "I've got an idea."

Sarah handed them over. Lily took out the Rose Quartz and fitted it into the necklace, then she slipped it over her head. A sparkling pink light filled the cave. Just looking at it made Ava feel calmer and happier. *The Peace Crystal*, she thought.

Lily spread her hands to show she wasn't a threat. "Please don't worry, I'm not going to do anything to you or Mai," she said, approaching the gargoyle slowly. "I think you understand me, don't you? You knew what Mai was talking about when she was saying she was scared or didn't like things."

The gargoyle nodded.

Lily stepped closer. The gargoyle gave a hiss but it sounded less threatening this time.

"I just want to help," Lily said. Watching the gargoyle closely for its reaction, she reached out and put her hand tentatively on its arm.

Ava held her breath as the gargoyle tensed but then it slowly relaxed, the suspicion fading from its face as the Rose Quartz's magic flowed from Lily into it. Its glittering eyes grew softer and then it covered Lily's hand with its own gnarled fingers, its claws retracting like a cat's.

"Thank you for looking after Mai," Lily said softly. "You've been a brilliant guardian but you don't need to protect her any more. I'm her sister. That's my job."

The gargoyle studied Lily for a long moment
and then its wings furled and it stepped back,
away from Mai. Lily leaned forward and
brushed her sister's hair away from her face.
"She's fine," she said, looking round at the
others. "You were right, Ava. She's just asleep."

"How are we going to get her home?" Sarah
said.

The gargoyle pointed at Mai and then at
himself. "I think the gargoyle's going to help us,"
said Lily with a smile.

The gargoyle lifted Mai up and carried her through the tunnels. When they reached the cave with four tunnels, it headed for one leading north. "That's not the way for us," Sarah said quickly. "We can't use the tower like you can. We have to go this way." She pointed to the tunnel leading to the west.

The gargoyle pointed at Mai then himself and then upwards and gave Lily a questioning look.

Lily understood. "Yes, please fly Mai home. Thank you."

"How did you know which tunnel was the right one for us?" said Ava to Sarah as the gargoyle nodded and set off down the north tunnel.

Sarah shone her torch at a little pyramid of stones beside the entrance to the south tunnel. "I marked each of the tunnels as we came through them."

"Sarah, you Rock!" Ava said with a grin.

"Just call me Rock Girl," said Sarah proudly.

She frowned. "Hmm. Maybe not."

"I don't know. Karate Kid and Rock Girl has a certain ring," said Ava.

"Excuse me, don't forget Ballet Flop," said Lily, mock-indignantly.

"Karate Kid, Rock Girl and Ballet Flop – we always save the day!" said Ava.

"Woof!" said Pepper.

"And their Tibetan Terror too of course." Ava grinned, ruffling Pepper's head.

Chuckling, the girls set off down the tunnel that led home.

*

It was wonderful to finally climb out of the dank darkness. Ava felt a rush of relief as she shut the trapdoor and they went up the cellar steps, ducking under the cobwebs, and emerged into the kitchen. They'd left the light on and the room was bright and cheerful.

Ava glanced at the kitchen clock. It felt like

they'd been out half the night but only an hour and a half had passed. If they were really lucky, maybe they'd be able to get back to Lily's before Jasmine realized they'd gone.

"We'd better go now," she said.

"Yes, I really want to see Mai and make sure she's OK," said Lily.

As they opened the door of the moonlit Curio Room, something landed on the window ledge. It was the gargoyle. It ducked in through the open window.

Pepper trotted over and reached up to sniff noses with it, her curly tail wagging over her back. It sniffed her nose then reached out and patted her head gently. Pepper looked slightly surprised but then she licked the gargoyle.

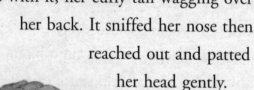

"Is Mai all right?" Lily asked it anxiously.

The gargoyle's fierce mouth spread into a smile as it put its hands together against one cheek and mimed sleep. Then, with a flap of its wings, it took off and flew to the shelves, landing on the bottom one. Its wings folded flat against its body and it settled into a comfortable position.

"We'd better send its spirit back to sleep," said Lily, getting the crystals out. "Should we use the Osiris Stone?" Gingerly she took a large stone out of the box – one side was white and the other was black. It had the power to wake spirits up or send them back to sleep.

"Do we have to?" Ava said. Now she knew the gargoyle wasn't dangerous, she was quite fond of it.

The gargoyle beckoned to Lily and held out its hands.

"I think it wants us to," said Lily.

She gently put the stone into the gargoyle's

cupped hands, black side down so it touched its palms. The gargoyle sighed happily and then they saw the glittering light in its eyes dim as it turned back to stone once again.

"Thank you," Lily whispered, kissing its head.

CHAPTER TWELVE

When they got back to Lily's house, they went in through the back door, took their coats and shoes off in the kitchen and then tiptoed past the lounge where Jasmine was working.

"Hey, you three!"

They froze.

"You should be in bed by now," said Jasmine. "I was just about to come and check on you. Were you getting a snack?"

"Y-yes," said Lily.

"OK, well off you go now," said Jasmine.

"And don't talk for too long."

"We won't," they chorused.

"Phew!" said Ava as they headed up the stairs. "That was close."

"It looks like we got away with it, though!" said Sarah.

Lily paused by Mai's door and turned the handle. Mai was fast asleep in her bed, the duvet tucked around her, one hand still clasping the Jade Crystal. Lily went over and gently took it out of her fingers. She slipped it into her pocket.

"Night, Mai," she whispered, smoothing back a strand of her sister's hair.

Mai's eyes blinked open sleepily. "Lily?"

"Yes, it's me," Lily said.

"I was having such weird dreams," said Mai. "The monster got me but it turned out to be a nice monster."

"They're the best kind," Lily said, smiling.

Mai pushed herself up in bed. "And I was dreaming about you. We were doing the theatre class but you were really unhappy. You said you hated it."

"I did hate it. I know you like acting and singing but I don't," said Lily.

Mai looked puzzled. "So why did you come?"

"Because you wanted me to," said Lily.

"Oh." Mai frowned then she reached out and stroked Lily's hand. "I love you, Lily. I'll tell Mummy you don't have to come with me any more," she went on, drowsily. "I'll be OK. Cici will be there."

"Cici seems nice," Ava said.

"Maybe you could be best friends with her," suggested Sarah. "Like me, Ava and Lily are."

Mai considered it for a moment and then nodded. She snuggled down under her duvet again. "Night," she yawned.

"Night," Lily said softly, backing out of the room. By the time she got to the doorway, Mai was asleep.

Lily shut the door and gave the others a delighted smile. "No more theatre class for me!"

"Which means more time for magic!" said Ava.

Sarah linked arms with them both. "Everything's worked out perfectly, after all!"

*

The girls were woken the next morning by Mai bouncing into their room. "Wake up! It's snowed again!"

They jumped up and looked out the window.

The world was covered with a thick blanket of pristine snow.

"I wish our sledges weren't broken," said Mai.

"We don't need sledges to go sledging!" said Ava. "Come on!"

An hour later, they were tramping up a snowy hill carrying four bodyboards that Ava had noticed in the shed.

Cai helped Mai climb the hill while Lily's dad built a snowman with Huy at the bottom. "Mai says you don't want to go to the theatre class," Cai said to Lily as they struggled up the hill through the thick snow.

"I don't," Lily admitted. "I didn't like it at all. I knew I wouldn't."

"I'll go with Cici, Mummy!" said Mai, waving to Cici who had just arrived at the bottom of the slope.

"Oh, Lily, I thought you didn't mind going," Cai said, looking at her older daughter. "Next time, please tell me how you're feeling, OK?"

"I will, Mum," Lily said with a smile. "I promise."

Her mum smiled back at her.

"Can I go down the hill now, Mummy?" said Mai impatiently. "I want to get to Cici!"

"All right," said Cai settling her on the bodyboard. "But hold on to the sides and don't go too fast. You can't steer on this thing!"

Mai didn't listen. She pushed herself off hard and whizzed down the slope. "Wheee!" she shouted. Luckily her dad was there at the bottom to catch her.

"Our turn now!" said Ava, grinning at the others.

She, Sarah and Lily lined up their makeshift sledges. Pepper jumped on to the bodyboard in front of Ava.

"Are you all ready?" Cai said to them.

"Ready!" they cried. Cai gave them each a firm push and they set off down the slope, the bodyboards speeding over the thick snow. Pepper's ears flew out behind her and she woofed in delight. Ava felt an explosion of happiness as the cold air stung her cheeks and the snow crystals flew up around them as they shot down the hill beside Sarah and Lily. She was so glad she had moved to Curio House, so glad she had made best friends with Sarah and Lily, but most of all she was so glad that her life was full of magic.

It's brilliant being a magic keeper! she thought.

Meanwhile, back in the Curio Room, a ray of winter sunshine stole in through the windows. A metal curio glittered brightly for a few seconds. The sun went behind a cloud but in the silent room, the curio continued to glow...

Look out for the
Magic Keepers' next
adventure in...

MAGIC KEEPERS
MYSTERIOUS MISHAPS

Also by Linda Chapman

Also by Linda Chapman

ABOUT THE AUTHOR

Linda Chapman is the best-selling
author of over 200 books. The biggest
compliment Linda can receive is for a
child to tell her they became a reader after
reading one of her books.

Linda lives in a cottage with a tower in
Leicestershire with her husband, three
children, three dogs and two ponies.
When she's not writing, Linda likes to
ride, read and visit schools and libraries to
talk to people about writing.

www.lindachapmanauthor.co.uk

ABOUT THE ILLUSTRATOR

Giang has been working as a children's
book illustrator for more than ten years.
She works in a studio with her partner
and three cats. She also loves comics and
graphic novels, and dreams of one day
finding the time to make her own comic
series. Nowadays she tries to practise yoga
so that she can keep her back fine after
a long time of it being not so fine.